TUNNEL

W9-DGI-772

STAY AWAKE...

Read
INSOMNIACS

1 ROAD KILL
2 FROZEN
3 TALK TO ME
4 TUNNEL

S.R. Martin

INSOMNIACS

TUNNEL

SCHOLASTIC INC.
New York Toronto London Auckland Sydney
Mexico City New Delhi Hong Kong

If you purchased this book without a cover, you should be aware that this book is stolen property. It was reported as "unsold and destroyed" to the publisher, and neither the author nor the publisher has received any payment for this "stripped book."

No part of this publication may be reproduced in whole or in part, or stored in a retrieval system or transmitted in any form or by any means, electronic, mechanical, photocopying, recording, or otherwise, without written permission of the publisher. For information regarding permission, write to Scholastic Australia Pty Limited, ACN 000 614 577, PO Box 579, Gosford 2250, Australia.

ISBN 0-590-69149-X

Copyright © 1997 by S.R. Martin.

All rights reserved. Published by Scholastic Inc., 555 Broadway, New York, NY 10012, by arrangement with Scholastic Australia Pty Limited.

SCHOLASTIC and associated logos are trademarks and/or registered trademarks of Scholastic Inc.

12 11 10 9 8 7 6 5 4 3 2 1   9/9 0 1 2 3 4/0

Printed in the U.S.A.

First Scholastic printing, May 1999

1 CHAPTER ONE

People are always reminding me that there's supposed to be a light at the end of the tunnel.

I never nod when they say this, and this seems to upset or confuse them, so they tend to go into long explanations about having a positive attitude and facing up to adversity.

Of course, they never say which tunnel is supposed to have a light at its end. In fact, I think a lot of them have never been in a tunnel, so they actually know squat about what they're talking about.

You see, I've been in a tunnel. And the tunnel I was in had no light at the end of it.

My tunnel had no end at all.

The complex where I live with my parents is called Greenbriars. It's situated about sixty miles south of Perth and has been built over what used to be a light industrial area. As the population of the city grew, more and more land on its outskirts was reclaimed as suburbs. The industries were moved farther south and the land they'd occupied bulldozed to make way for the developers and their project homes.

I suppose Greenbriars started out as a good idea. Once the developers had leveled the land, they'd then gone and planted trees along all the streets to give the impression that the area was lush and cool and inviting. They'd even been clever enough to sell most of the homes during the winter months, so the feeling you got when you came into the area was of acres of greenery with these picturesque little houses tucked away behind trees.

Unfortunately, after everyone had bought and moved in, winter moved through spring and into summer. And summer in Perth means water restrictions. The instant lawns the developers had planted died and weeds took their place. The trees along the roadsides withered away, and what we were left with was your basic desertlike outer suburb.

It's pretty damn ugly, to tell the truth. The only thing green about it is the name of the estate.

But, to be honest, at the time we moved in,

I really didn't care about things like that. To me it was a new place full of things I hadn't seen or done, so whenever I had the chance I'd be out the back door, over the fence, and off exploring.

2
CHAPTER TWO

I met Alex and Ken one Saturday morning.

My parents had gone off shopping for the weekly groceries, taking my loudly complaining younger brother along with them. Poor Mike always wanted to be left behind with me, but Mom and Dad figured he was too young to go wandering around with just his older brother to look after him.

"You're only five, Michael," Mom used to say. "When you're a little older and know more about who you can trust and who you can't, we'll let you go play with Matthew."

"But Matthew can look after me," Mike would complain.

"He's got enough trouble just looking after himself," Dad would growl, and that would be the end of that.

I didn't mind looking after Mike, even though he can be kind of a hassle at times, but Dad was right. When I'm interested in doing something, I seem to lose all interest in anything else. There was a definite possibility that I'd forget I had Mike in tow, and by the time I remembered he'd probably be miles away, screaming his head off and wetting his pants.

He certainly didn't know the complex well enough to find his way home if we got separated.

10

*   *   *

I'd been wandering up and down the dusty streets for half an hour or so, not really heading anywhere in particular, when I turned down a cul-de-sac that only had a couple of houses at the start of it. There was half a house a bit farther down, where someone had started to build but then run out of money, and past that there was a small grove of eucalyptus trees that had been overlooked by the developers' bulldozer.

After spending some time in the shell of the incomplete house, rummaging around for scraps of pipe and tin that I could try to sell at the recycling center, I strolled down to the trees. They were the first green things I'd seen around since the coming of summer, so for that reason alone they were interesting.

As I got a little closer, however, they became more interesting.

There was a banging noise. Or at least

that's what I thought it was. It started like a low, drawn-out cry. Then it would increase in pitch until it became like a shout, and finally end with a loud, sharp *whack*. I thought it might have been some sort of machinery.

Moving into the trees I was surrounded by that hot, dry smell of baked sand and dead leaves. Looking down, I could see bull ants pouring around my feet to join some others who were dragging along a large grasshopper. I leaned down to get a closer look. Then I started to hear voices.

I continued through the trees until they suddenly gave way to an area which was entirely concrete. It stretched away from me for hundreds of yards, and standing in the middle of it were two boys holding a sledgehammer.

They were hard to see at first because the heat on the concrete was causing those wet-looking shimmers to happen, and for a second or so I thought they were actually stand-ing in midair.

As they'd seen me the moment I emerged from the trees, I continued to walk toward them. If I'd tried to duck back into hiding they would have known I was trying to spy on them and would have probably come right over and proceeded to give me a good pounding.

"Facing up to it," my father is fond of say-ing, "is the first step in winning anything."

I wasn't trying to win anything, but I faced them anyway.

"Hey, guys, whatcha doin'?" I asked as I got close to them.

They stared at me for a moment, then the one with the sledgehammer cleared his throat, spat an enormous spit wad on the ground in front of him, and said, "Smashin' things. What's it to you?"

I started grinning.

*   *   *

I'm pretty fond of smashing things myself.

Not other people's property, though I guess anything that's not mine must, in effect, be someone else's. But rather, stuff that's been discarded and left to fall apart.

I mean, if it's falling apart, what harm is there in helping it along the way?

Alex and Ken were taking turns at trying to smash a hole through the concrete. Or in reality Alex, who was the larger of the two, was trying to smash the hole. Ken was providing encouragement. The long, drawn-out cry I'd heard earlier was the sound Alex made swinging the heavy sledgehammer over his head.

"Why here?" I asked. As far as I could see they could have smashed a hole anywhere on the concrete slab. They even could have started over near the trees where there'd be some shade.

14

"Once we've made a hole, we're going to dig underneath it," Ken replied.

I must have looked as if I didn't understand.

"So we can make a room under the concrete," he continued. "It'll be our place, a sort of home away from home."

"You live in the complex?" I asked.

"Ken still does, sometimes," Alex said rather sulkily, and the two of them started snickering. "I live where I want to nowadays."

"Alex doesn't get along with his parents that well," Ken continued. "So we're making him a home. I might come and live here, too."

We stood around for a few seconds sizing one another up.

"I've lived here for a couple of months," I said. "Haven't seen you two before."

"We haven't seen you, either," Alex said,

15

trying to stare me down. "So we're just about equal."

"Well, if that's the case," I said, reaching out for the sledgehammer, "maybe I can have a turn with that?"

Alex looked over at Ken, who nodded.

It took us a couple of hours to smash a hole big enough to function as a doorway. Or really, it took Alex and me a couple of hours. Ken stood at the sidelines and made suggestions.

During that time they explained to me that the concrete slab had been the floor of an old slaughterhouse that had been demolished by the developers. It was supposed to be part of the next stage of the estate, so they'd eventually clear away the concrete slab as well. Smashing a few holes in it wouldn't matter one way or the other.

It was hot work and the concrete was old and thick, but we managed it.

We cleared out the rubble and were left with a hole about a yard across, underneath which there was rich black soil.

"That looks pretty easy to dig through," Ken said. "Shouldn't take us too long at all."

"What are we going to do with the soil?" I asked.

"What do you mean?"

"Well," I said rather carefully, because Alex was glaring at me as if I'd just tried to tell him he was stupid or something, and he was still holding the sledgehammer, which I'd noticed he could handle pretty deftly, "if we just pile it up around the hole, anyone who comes by will know that there's something happening here, won't they? Do you want people to know where you're living?"

Alex glanced across at Ken again, who

scratched his head and started to look around.

"Matthew's right," he said eventually. He looked at me. "Got any suggestions?"

"Yes, as a matter of fact. If we bring some buckets when we start the digging we can carry the soil over to the trees there." I pointed back the way I'd come. "We can scatter it around and no one'll know the difference."

Ken nodded. "Buckets it is, then."

3 CHAPTER THREE

When I got home late for lunch that day I must have looked quite a mess because my mother rolled her eyes and tut-tutted at me, though my father seemed to think I looked rather funny.

"You been practicing to be a construction worker or something?" he chuckled.

"Go and get yourself cleaned up," my mother said, shaking her head.

Mike pouted and said nothing. It was obvious he hadn't enjoyed the morning's shopping and was envious of the fact that I'd been out doing something that had caused me to get very dirty.

In the bathroom mirror I looked like a bomb blast victim, covered in gray concrete dust and with a tiny trickle of blood running down my left cheek where one of the flying chips from the concrete must have struck me. I washed up and came out for lunch, which was tuna salad, probably my least favorite dish in the world, but something my parents said was practical and healthy.

"What on earth were you up to, Matthew?" my mother asked as I picked through my lunch.

"I met some guys. We're working on a project."

"What guys? What project?"

"Leave him alone, hon," my father suggested. "He's made some friends, that's all. They're doing boys' things. Let him have his secrets."

I was grateful for the intervention. For some reason the thought of telling my mother that I'd met a couple of guys — one of whom lived on the streets — and that we'd been smashing holes in concrete so we could dig a big hole underneath it where they could live didn't really seem like a good idea.

"You know that old bucket you've got in the shed, Dad? The one you mix the lawn fertilizer in?"

"What about it?" Dad said around a mouthful of canned fish and cherry tomatoes.

"You think I can borrow it for a while?"

"What for?"

"Now, now, dear," Mom suddenly piped up. "Let him have his secrets."

23

Dad looked at her, grinned, and shrugged his shoulders.

I took the bucket with me the next day. We'd agreed to meet in the morning at around eight so that we could get a lot of the digging done before it got too hot.

The day before, Alex and I had gotten soaked swinging the sledgehammer, and even Ken had looked a bit hot and bothered on occasion.

We also knew that, being Sunday, there wouldn't be a lot of people around at that hour. They'd either be having lazy breakfasts over newspapers, mowing the lawns, going to church, or sleeping in.

That's the good thing about Sundays, they're very private.

The digging was reasonably easy, so even Ken joined in. And after only an hour we had made a depression underneath the shattered rim of concrete that was big enough to crouch in. It was extremely cool once you got out of the direct sunlight, though there was a slight smell coming from the earth that was sour and faintly nauseating.

"What a stench," I muttered as I heaved a bucket of soil up to Alex, who had the unfortunate task of hauling the heavy bucket across the hundred yards or so of hot concrete to the trees, where he'd scatter it around.

"That's nothing," he sneered at me. "You try sleeping in between the Dumpsters behind a Kentucky Fried Chicken for a night and see what you say about stench then."

I gathered Alex had had a pretty tough life, but I didn't want to question him about it too much. He seemed pretty defensive and I didn't really want to get on his bad side (not that he seemed to have much of a good one, for that matter).

The farther down we dug, the worse the smell became, but because the other two didn't complain about it neither did I. It was their hole, after all. I was just a someone who wanted some company.

We dug until lunchtime, then I raced back home for a quick bite. It's amazing what digging a large hole can do for your appetite.

Alex and Ken looked a little upset when I said I was going off to eat, and I realized it was because neither of them had lunches waiting for them at home. Alex didn't even have a home.

"You want me to try and bring something back for you?" I asked.

Alex's eyes lit up, but Ken shook his head.

"We don't need your charity," he said, rather sulkily, I thought.

Alex looked as if he were going to empty the full bucket of soil he was holding all over Ken's head.

4 CHAPTER FOUR

"**Y**ou smell like something that died by the side of the road," Mike said to me when I walked in.

"And you look like something the cat coughed up after licking itself," I replied as I went into the bathroom to clean up.

Little brothers can be really annoying at times, but he was right about the smell. It was pretty bad and it seemed to cling to my clothes. I could get it off my skin by scrubbing it with soap, but I had to change into old jeans and a fresh shirt before coming out to lunch.

My mother looked at my clothes and I could see a question forming, but she thought better of it.

Dad had brought back some fish and chips for lunch, which is a favorite of mine. I wolfed them down so fast I don't think I chewed anything, and I'd even started eyeing Mike's half-eaten piece of fish when I got a sudden attack of guilt.

I remembered the look on Alex's face when Ken said that they didn't need me to bring them back anything to eat. Apart from the fact that he was angry, he actually looked hungry as well. And I don't just mean the sort of hungry you get when you're late for a regular meal. This was real hunger. You could see it staring out from behind his eyes.

Surprising everyone, I took the four plates we'd been using and did the washing up. (We always eat our takeout on plates. Mom thinks it's "cheap" not to.)

When I was sure no one was going to walk into the kitchen, I opened the fridge and rummaged around inside, constructing two clumsy — but massive — tuna fish sandwiches from yesterday's leftovers. I hoped Alex and Ken didn't have the same aversion to canned fish that I did.

Because I didn't have anything to carry them in, I had to stuff both sandwiches down my shirt and leave the house with my hands clutched across my stomach so no one would see.

I didn't have to worry, though. Mom and Dad didn't even look up from the afternoon movie they were watching, and Mike was nowhere to be seen.

*   *   *

The look on Alex's face was worth bottling. Because Ken had said they didn't need my charity, he stuck by his guns and refused the sandwich I'd made him, so Alex ate them both.

In about five seconds flat. Four bites. Four swallows. That was that.

He even thanked me, which I gathered was something very rare because one of Ken's eyebrows went up so far I thought it was trying to crawl into his hairline.

We worked through the afternoon, digging, hauling, and scattering.

There was a rhythm to what we were doing that joined the three of us, somehow seeming to make us all closer. Even though we were dog-tired and covered in sweat, every time we'd look one another in the eyes it brought a smile to everyone's face, and we'd always be cracking jokes and competing among ourselves to see who could work the fastest.

By the time I was ready to call it quits, we were all friends. Close friends.

I know it sounds strange to say it, but that stinking hole underneath the floor of the old slaughterhouse joined us as firmly as if we'd all been born from the same mother, and I went home knowing that I'd stick by Alex and Ken no matter what.

And vice versa.

5 CHAPTER FIVE

Because it was only a week before school started again for the year, Mom took me shopping the next morning for books and clothes and all the usual stuff that goes with our compulsory education.

"If I have to go to school," I used to complain, "how come you have to pay for it as well?"

Mom gave me one of those looks that could be interpreted two ways: either "Don't ask me questions I can't answer" or "Ask your father. He thinks he knows everything."

Sensibly, I chose not to take either option.

It was already two o'clock by the time we got home, and then I was forced through all the usual indignities of having to parade the new clothes we'd bought in front of the rest of the family. It made me feel like a motorized store dummy. Especially with Mike sneering away in the background — he'd had to go through the same thing a week before when Mom had bought his uniform for his first year of school, so he was getting back at me.

I guess I didn't blame him, but that wouldn't stop me from getting my revenge later on that night.

Maybe I can plan something especially unpleasant with Alex and Ken this afternoon, I thought as I turned around in the startlingly white shirt and gray twill pants my mother said made me look so grown-up and handsome.

When I finally got to the hole it was the hottest part of the day, and I was looking forward to the cool underneath the concrete.

It appeared, however, that Alex and Ken had gone. I'd seen a lot of fresh soil scattered about among the trees when I'd passed through them, but when I stuck my head down the hole I couldn't see a thing outside the circle of light thrown by the entrance. I called out their names but got no answer.

They'd made a lot of progress, though. The floor now looked like it was nearly six feet down and I had no idea how wide it was from wall to wall. Also, the smell was a lot stronger. Having been away from it for a while, it made me really wrinkle up my nose.

I sat up and looked around but could see no sign of the others. The sun was beating down and I could feel beads of sweat break-ing out all over my body and trickling down from my armpits.

"Forget this," I said out loud, and got up to leave.

That's when I heard the sound. It was like a far-off rumble. So far off, in fact, that I wasn't sure I heard it at all.

I listened for a minute but didn't hear any-thing else, so I started to leave again. Then — quite distinctly this time — I heard a definite moaning sound. It wasn't the same as the rumble I heard before, but it was a lot closer. The only problem was, it didn't sound human. It also sounded like it was coming from behind me.

Very slowly, I turned around.

There was nothing there except for the hole. I stared at it for a while but didn't hear the sound again. I did, however, get a defi-nite case of goose bumps even though it was sweltering hot, and when a car backfired a couple of blocks away I jumped a good foot.

"This is stupid," I said, out aloud again. "Alex? Ken? You down there?" I called to the hole, and realized at the same time how silly I probably looked standing in the middle of a massive stretch of concrete shouting at the ground.

I lay down and stuck my head and shoulders as far into the hole as they would go, trying to peer into the darkness. It was, however, impenetrable.

"Alex? Ken?" I was whispering by this stage.

Again, nothing.

There was something about the darkness that bothered me, but I couldn't quite put my finger on what it was. It was almost as if the darkness was too dark, if you know what I mean, just a shade too far beyond black.

No amount of peering or closing my eyes so they'd adjust could make me see any farther than the *Star Trek*-like cone of light I had my head in.

I shook my head, as much at my own stupidity as anything else, and started to heave my upper body out of the hole.

That's when there was an enormous bellow and I felt myself being dragged — shrieking at the top of my lungs — off the lip of the hole and into the stinking darkness.

CHAPTER SIX

After I'd called them every name I knew under the sun — and quite a few I didn't even know I knew — Alex and Ken eventually stopped laughing and lit some torches they'd made and stuck into the earth walls.

It put a different perspective on things.

Apart from the fact that it was quite damp and stank to high heaven, the room underneath the concrete was quite homey. They'd scored a couple of old chairs from somewhere and stuck them in the corners and made a table of sorts from milk crates and a slab of plywood. There was a bundle of bedding rolled up in one corner, which I presumed belonged to Alex, and, rather oddly, I thought, a framed picture of the queen of England held in place on one wall by sticks jammed into the soil.

The light from the torches gave the place a flickering glow that made the walls dance slightly, and every now and then the picture of the queen looked as if it were dancing along with them.

"What do you think?" asked Alex excitedly.

"I think you're both dog vomit," I said shakily.

"Not us, you twerp, the cave," Ken continued.

"Is that what you're calling it now, a cave?"

"What else would you call it?" Alex said.

"A stinking big hole in the ground." I grinned when I said this, so they knew I was joking.

I thought the cave was great. It was better than great, actually; it was sensational. They'd done an enormous amount in the time I'd been away shopping with Mom.

"I'm sleeping here tonight," Alex said proudly. "It's my home now, and no one else is to know about it."

"Our home," Ken corrected him. "We all built it, so it's all of ours."

I murmured my agreement and Alex nodded along with us.

"This is great," I said.

We spent the rest of the afternoon widening the hole even farther. One of us would wait outside on the concrete while another would stand on one of the crates to pass up the bucket of soil.

After we'd gotten the main room to the size we wanted, we planned to start digging tunnels off in different directions, opening up other rooms as we went.

"We'll make it like a maze down here," Ken said, "with different entrances and everything. We could even tunnel over to the trees and have a special escape route."

"What are we going to be escaping from?" I asked.

Ken didn't have an answer to that.

As we worked, the sky through the hole in the concrete changed from that blue-white color you get on really hot days, through deeper shades of blue until it became gray.

I threw my bucket in the corner.

"That's it for me," I said, wiping sweat from my brow with the back of my hand. "I'll be back first thing tomorrow and we can start tunneling. I'll try and bring some food and stuff. You know, supplies for us."

We were all excited with what we'd ac-complished, and Alex, who had been out-side carrying the dirt over to the trees, gave a huge whoop of excitement and leaped down through the hole to join Ken and me.

And, in complete silence, went straight through the floor.

Ken and I stood looking at the Alex-sized hole that appeared between us for about half a second, quickly glanced up at each other, and then both let out yells as the floor underneath us gave way as well.

7

CHAPTER SEVEN

It was dark.

Very, very dark.

And sticky.

When I moved I could hear a wet, sucking sound as my body came away from the ground. It felt like I had landed in a few inches of half-congealed glue.

Glue that stank really badly.

I held my hand up to my face and

only realized I couldn't see it when I felt it touch and stick to my cheek.

With quite some effort, I managed to sit up.

Slowly I ran my hands over my body to feel if I was all in one piece. As far as I could tell, I was. Even though I was in some pain, it was no worse than anything I'd encountered on the soccer field. At least there were no bones sticking out from odd places. It was impossible to tell if I was bleeding because everything felt so sticky, and I couldn't smell blood because everything smelled so overwhelmingly disgusting anyway.

I guessed I was all right.

That's when I turned my head to the side and threw up in a great, stomach-cleansing heave.

"Oh, gross," a voice said in the darkness.

I froze.

"What was that?" another voice said.

"Someone just threw up all over my head," the first voice replied.

"That's got to be Matthew," the voice I now recognized as Ken's said.

"Oh, fine. That makes it all right, then," came Alex's rather indignant reply. "Why don't you take a turn now, Ken?"

"I just might, since it's your fault we're here. Wherever here happens to be," Ken snarled.

"Hey, guys," I called into the darkness. "Can you can the slapstick until we know what's going on?"

I moved around until I was on all

fours and stuck one hand out in front of me. It encountered something which leapt away from me with a "yeep" of terror and a distinct breaking of wind.

"What was that?" I cried.

"What was what?" came Alex and Ken in unison.

"I just touched something and it farted and ran away."

"Had to be Ken," came Alex's voice.

"Well, you wouldn't sit still either, if something suddenly jabbed you in the back, would you? It isn't exactly user-friendly down here." Ken's voice rose until it reached a point of near hysteria.

Then the two of them really went at it, each screaming at the other, accusing each other of crimes I'd never even heard of, all in high-pitched, shaky voices that sounded more terrified than angry.

It took me bellowing at the top of my voice to calm them, and even then one of them would let out a sniffle or grunt of disapproval every now and then. The first thing I decided we had to do was locate one another properly.

"Okay, let's move toward one another's voices and try and link arms. That way we'll know who's who and we won't lose anyone," I said in as commanding a voice as I could muster.

"How are we going to lose anyone?" Ken asked nervously.

"When we try and get out of here, idiot," Alex shouted.

"I'm staying here until someone finds us," Ken continued.

"No one's going to find us, Ken," I said. "My parents don't know where I am, your parents don't care, and Alex doesn't have parents as far as I know. Who's going to find us? All anyone will see is a flat stretch of concrete without anyone on it. They're not going to go searching the surface for holes, are they? Now both of you move toward my voice."

I heard the sound of them squelching through the muck on the floor, then I received a sharp jab in the eye with someone's finger.

"Ow!"

"Ah, found you," came Alex's satisfied chuckle. "Come on, dog vomit, we're over here."

"Don't call me that." Ken's voice was right in my ear.

We all linked arms in the darkness. Now that we were all together, I was at something of a loss as to what to do. All I knew was that it was comforting to feel my friends close by, no matter how irritating they were in the present situation.

"Where do you think we are, Matthew?" Alex suddenly asked. He was so close to me I nearly jumped out of my skin when he spoke.

"I guess it's something to do with the slaughterhouse. Maybe the drains underneath it. I think what happened was that all our jumping in and out of the hole weakened whatever was the roof of this place, and that final jump you made, Alex, was the straw that broke the camel's back."

"The what that broke whose back?" Ken mumbled. "And if this is an old slaughterhouse drain, what is all this sticky stuff we're sitting in?"

There was silence for a few seconds, then Alex worked it out.

"Oh, gross."

"What?" said Ken. "Someone throw up on your head again?"

"No, but I've got an idea of what we're sitting in."

"What?"

"You really don't want to know."

"If it's a drain," I said, to stop the conversation going the way I knew it would, "then it's got to have an exit. We should start moving."

"Oh yeah," came Ken's sarcastic

snarl. "And which direction would you suggest, Doctor Livingstone?"

"I don't care which way we head," Alex said before I could reply. "As long as we're moving, I'm happy. I really don't want to sit around here listening to you whining."

"Hold on to my shirt," I said as I leaned forward and started crawling.

CHAPTER EIGHT

I have no idea how far we moved through the drain. It seemed like it went on forever.

By standing up and holding hands we were able to work out that it was about three yards wide, because we could just touch both walls if we all stretched out. That meant it was the same height, so there was no way we would ever reach the roof. It did mean that we could stand up, though, which was a whole lot better than crawling through the muck.

It was still completely dark, and no matter how long we stayed down there my vision didn't adjust at all. I still couldn't see my fingers in front of my face. At least there was nothing in the drain to trip us up, and we continued on in single file, with me in the lead, followed by Alex and then Ken. Our only company was the sound of our feet sucking in and out of the sticky stuff on the floor.

"It's old blood, isn't it?" Alex suddenly whispered in my ear. "The sticky stuff. We're walking through old blood."

"Don't be ridiculous," I whispered back. "If it's blood, it would have dried up years ago."

"Not if it's always been damp down here," he continued. "It would just congeal like a thick jelly or something."

"Shut up, Alex," I hissed.

"What are you two whispering about?" Ken whined from the back of the line. "I don't like it when you whisper. It's creepy enough down here as it is."

"You are such a wuss," Alex snapped at him. "We're just stuck in a drain, that's all. There's nothing to be so scared about."

That's when we heard the sound.

It was a long, low moan, and it sounded like it was coming from far down the drain in front of us.

I stopped dead still and Alex and Ken crashed into me from behind.

There was silence for several seconds, then we heard the sound again, far off and low and mournful.

In one swift movement, every single hair on my body stood up on end, quivering to attention like soldiers on parade.

"I thought you said there was nothing to be scared about," whispered Ken.

"There isn't," Alex said, but he was whispering now, too. "That's just the wind or something."

"What wind?" Ken continued, and I had to agree with him. It was dead still, which made the sound even creepier.

The sound came again, slightly closer this time.

"Is it me, or does that sound closer?" Alex whispered.

"Who's the wuss now?" I heard Ken say.

"Maybe we should go back the way we came?" I suggested, and immediately felt Alex start to turn around.

"Good idea, Matthew."

Then the sound came again, much closer this time, and with it the air suddenly became very cold.

"See," I said, "it's just the wind."

"If it was the wind, Matthew," Alex said, tugging me along with him, "it would be moving, wouldn't it? This isn't moving, it's just getting colder."

9
CHAPTER NINE

I'm not sure who broke into a run first, but the next second we were pelting down the drain at full speed, stumbling and cursing ourselves and one another, trying madly not to fall into the muck on the floor (which is not easy in total darkness while holding hands with two other guys who are panicking as much as you are).

At one point an earsplitting scream sounded right next to me, but it was just Ken giving voice to the feelings that I was also having. We had no idea what the sound behind us was at that stage, only that it was coming closer and that it made us all feel extremely frightened. Also, the closer the sound came, the larger it became, almost as if more and more sounds were being added to it.

Every now and then we'd all career into one side of the drain or the other, tumbling over ourselves and screaming at the top of our lungs. We never let go of one another, though. I think the fear of being cut off from the other two was enough for our hands to lock permanently in place, and in the back of my mind was the thought that whenever we got out of here I'd have the imprint of Alex's hand on mine for the rest of my life.

It was Ken who finally lost contact.

We'd all taken another tumble and gone for a roll through the muck, gagging and cursing. I jumped to my feet again and realized that I wasn't holding Alex's hand.

The sound, by this point, was extremely loud, seeming to fill the air around us with a shuddering vibration. It was literally roaring through the drain, almost pushing us in front of it with the sheer volume of noise. It was also freezing cold and I found myself shivering uncontrollably.

"ALEX!" I shouted. "KEN!"

There was no answer. And even if there had been, I'm not sure I would have heard it above the roaring. I pressed my hands over my ears to try and block out some of the sound and started to stagger in what I thought was the direction we'd been heading before we were separated.

And that's when I fell over Alex. Right over him and flat on my face into the mess on the floor. I didn't even have time to put my hands down to break my fall because they were firmly fixed over my ears trying to shut out the noise.

I saw my first light then, because the fall caused me to see stars.

Alex grabbed onto me. "KEN?" he shouted when he'd groped around and finally discovered where my ear was.

"It's me, Matthew. Where's Ken?"

"I can't find him. I thought I'd lost you, too. Help me find him."

Holding onto each other as tightly as possible, we groped around us in every direction we could, but there was no sign of Ken. He'd just disappeared into the dark.

Finally, we sat there in the darkness, holding on to each other and listening to the sound get louder and louder, feeling the air get even colder around us.

"I know what the sound is," Alex said into my ear.

"What?"

"Listen to it," he said. "Try and separate the sounds."

I tried, but all I could hear was the roaring.

"It's cattle," he finally said. "Lots of cattle running toward us. Like a stampede."

That's when I knew he'd cracked.

"There haven't been cattle around here for years, not since they closed down the slaughterhouse," I snapped at him. "It's a suburb, Alex. A housing estate. You don't get cattle in housing complexes."

"I know."

I felt him start to get up.

"Alex, what are you doing?"

"I'm going to find Ken. He won't be so scared when he finds out it's just cattle. They can't hurt you. I was on a farm once and they were kind of friendly. Curious, you know?"

"You can't just leave me here, Alex."

"Then come with me. We'll both find him."

"I'm not going back in there."

"Then wait here," he said. He let go of my hand. And that was the last I ever knew of Alex.

10 CHAPTER TEN

I waited for a long time, but neither Alex nor Ken came back.

The longer I waited, the more my mind began to play tricks on me, until I was sure that what Alex had said was the truth — it was cattle I was hearing, thousands of them, bellowing out their pain and fear and frustration as they followed us along the dark drain through the earth.

I could hear their breathing, the sound of their many hooves stampeding down through the years, all focused together in a long tunnel of sound.

By this point my hair was standing completely on end and my teeth were chattering frantically.

In the end, I gave up. I couldn't wait for them any longer. The volume of sound and the terror it was creating were too much for me, and I leaped to my feet and tried to run as far from that place as possible.

Naturally, because it was pitch-black, I had no idea where I was going or even if I was going away from the sound, but just to be up and moving felt better.

I stumbled and staggered for what seemed like miles, cloaked in darkness and fear. I was crying and screaming and beginning to hallucinate, because every now and then I was sure I'd see the massive head of a steer in front of me, its eyes rolling in fright and its throat spilling blood. Every time I looked hard, though, the image would disappear and I'd be back in total darkness.

Then, for one brief, blissful second I was in the air.

It was a strange feeling, for all of a sudden I knew I was out of the tunnel, though where I was I had no idea, just that the air was cleaner and I could smell water instead of old blood. And just for a fraction of a second I saw something glittering and beautiful, my mind registering that it was stars just before I plunged into water and passed out.

I ended up in a small creek. It must have been where the drain from the old slaughterhouse came out, but no one ever found it. Somehow I managed to get myself onto the bank somewhere and some joggers found me in the morning.

After I told everyone my story, they went back to see if they could find the end of the drain, but nothing was there.

I spent some time in the hospital, more for shock than the bruises and scrapes I'd received, and I had a difficult time explaining exactly what had happened.

For starters, my fall in the creek had washed me quite clean, so I can understand why people's expressions were doubtful when I told them about tunnels full of old blood and the deafening sound of stampeding cattle. They'd nod and say "yes, yes" but I knew they were thinking I was a little crazy or something.

It was a couple of days before they told me that the entire area of concrete where we'd built our underground home had collapsed, and there was nothing there now except a massive depression in the ground with a lot of concrete rubble at the bottom of it.

They never found Alex and Ken, either.

In fact, some people say that I invented them, because no one in the complex had ever heard of them.

But I know they were real.

89

*　　*　　*

I have white hair now, a result of my experience underground, and I've become a firm vegetarian. Occasionally I'll wander over to where the huge slab of concrete used to be, but they've filled it in and built houses on top of it. I've asked some of the kids who live there now if they ever hear anything strange at night, anything like cattle, but they shake their heads and walk away from me rather quickly.

Sometimes I have dreams about my two friends. Strange dreams in which I see them astride massive cattle with red eyes that thunder endlessly along dark tunnels under the earth.

I know they're down there somewhere. Down where the tunnels run into a darkness deeper than anything you could ever imagine.

S.R. MARTIN

S.R. Martin was born and grew up in the beachside suburbs of Perth, Australia. A fascination with the ocean led to an early career in marine biology, but this was cut short when he decided the specimens he collected looked better under an orange-and-cognac sauce than they did under a microscope. After even quicker careers in banking, teaching, and journalism, a wanderlust led him through most of Australia's capital cities and then on to periods of time living in Hong Kong, Taiwan, South Korea, the United Kingdom, and the United States. Returning to Australia, he settled for Melbourne and a career as a freelance writer. In addition to the Insomniacs series, S.R. Martin is the author of *Swampland*, coming soon from Scholastic.